Guy Parker-Rees

DYLAN

THE SHOPKEEPER

Hello, I'm Dotty Bug.
Let's join in with the story!

ALISON GREEN BOOKS

When it's a sunny day,
Dylan's ready to play.

But what kind of day was it today?
A sleepy, do-nothing day?

No way!

"Today," said Dylan, "is a day for being a shopkeeper, so that all my friends can come and buy things."

Dylan dived under his bed,
rummaged around,
and found . . .

Do YOU like going to the shops?

...a till that went **ding!** when you put money in it.

He also found some brilliant things to sell:
a cuddly toy with only one ear; an old bit
of red string; lots of odd socks, and a
couple of very old sticky toffees.

What would YOU buy
from Dylan's shop?

Dylan set up his shop and waited for people to come and buy things.

But nobody came – apart from some ants,

Can you follow the marching ants with your finger?

and they didn't stop to buy anything.

"Maybe Purple Puss will buy something," said Dylan.
So he put everything into his trolley and took
his shop to Purple Puss's house.

Purple Puss was
busy making pompoms.

"Look at my shop!" said Dylan.

Purple Puss was very excited –
but she didn't buy anything.

Please come to my shop

Have YOU ever made a pompom?

Instead she said, "I'm going to have
a shop, too. I can sell my pompoms."

"But having a shop was
my idea," said Dylan.
"I want my till to go **ding!**
when people buy things."

"Well, maybe Jolly Otter will
buy something," said Purple Puss.

So Dylan and Purple Puss
packed up their shops,

Please come
to my

What would YOU sell
if you had a shop?

and went to see Jolly Otter.

Jolly Otter was busy
baking cakes with Titchy Chick.

"Look at our shops!" said Dylan.

Jolly Otter and Titchy Chick
were very excited – but they
didn't buy anything.

Pompom
Shop

Instead Jolly Otter said,
"I'm going to have a shop, too.
I can sell my cakes."

"But having a shop was my idea,"
said Dylan. "I want my till to go ding!
when people buy things."

I love those
cherries. Do YOU?

"Well, I'm sure people will
come and buy things if we
wait," said Jolly Otter.

So they waited . . . and waited . . .

. . . but nobody came to buy anything.

Please come to my shop

It was Titchy Chick's nap time, and she fell asleep in Dylan's shop.

Do YOU like to have a nap sometimes?

Then Purple Puss said, "I really like cakes, Jolly Otter, but I haven't got any money. Can I buy all your cakes with my pompoms?"

"Of course!" said Jolly Otter. "But only if I can buy all your pompoms with my cakes!"

So Jolly Otter sold all his cakes to Purple Puss, and
Purple Puss sold all her pompoms to Jolly Otter.

Dylan didn't sell anything to anyone.

"But having a shop was my idea," said
Dylan. "I want my till to go ding!
when people buy things."

Poor Dylan!

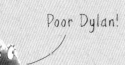

Just then, in swooped Crotchety Owl.
"An ant tells me a new shop has opened!"
she said. "I suppose it's just a lot of old rubbish."

She frowned at the
cuddly toy with one
ear missing,

and the old bit
of red string,

Do YOU think
Crotchety Owl
will buy anything?

and the pile of odd socks

and the very old sticky toffees,
and she said . . .

"Just what I need!
I'll buy the lot!"
And she handed Dylan
a big shiny coin.

Dylan was **very excited.**

He put the shiny coin
in his till, and the till went:

ding!

Hooray!

Then Crotchety Owl swooped away and
Dylan took his shiny coin out of his till.
"Now *I* want to buy something, but
there's nothing left," he said, sadly.

"You've sold all your pompoms and cakes
to each other, and Titchy Chick doesn't
have a shop at all."

Titchy Chick!
Where *was* Titchy Chick?

Do YOU know where Titchy Chick is?

"Oh, no!" said Dylan. "Crotchety Owl must have bought her with everything from my shop!"

They dashed off to Crotchety
Owl's tree to get her back.

Can YOU
run fast?

Crotchety Owl wasn't
looking crotchety at all.
"Look at my tree!" she said.

"The toffees were just the thing for holding up
my string of sock-bunting! I love my cuddly toy
– and I adore my yellow pompom!"

"But, Owl," said Dylan, "your yellow
pompom is our friend, Titchy Chick!
We have to take her back."

Oh, no!

Owl looked very sad.

"I could buy her back
with my shiny coin?"
said Dylan.

"I suppose so," said Owl.
"But she was the prettiest
thing in the tree."

"Poor Owl," said Dylan.

"How can we cheer her up?"

"We know what to do!"
said Purple Puss and Jolly Otter.

What do YOU think
they're going to do?

"A party!"
said Owl. "With
cake and pompoms!"

She gave such a happy hoot that she woke up Titchy Chick.

"Did you sell anything, Dylan?" asked Titchy Chick.

"Yes," said Purple Puss and Jolly Otter.
"He was the best shopkeeper ever!"

For Martha

First published in the UK in 2017 by
Alison Green Books
An imprint of Scholastic Children's Books
Euston House, 24 Eversholt Street
London NW1 1DB
A division of Scholastic Ltd
www.scholastic.co.uk
London – New York – Toronto – Sydney – Auckland
Mexico City – New Delhi – Hong Kong

Copyright © 2017 Guy Parker-Rees

HB ISBN: 978 1 407166 27 8
PB ISBN: 978 1 407166 28 5

The moral rights of Guy Parker-Rees have been asserted.

Papers used by Scholastic Children's Books are made from wood grown in sustainable forests.